Richard Stockham, Irving E. Cox

The Guardians & Perchance to Dream
(2 Dystopian Tales in One Edition)

OK Publishing 2021

Richard Stockham, Irving E. Cox

The Guardians & Perchance to Dream

(2 Dystopian Tales in One Edition)

Science Fiction Novellas

Published by

Books

- Advanced Digital Solutions & High-Quality book Formatting -

musaicumbooks@okpublishing.info

2021 OK Publishing

ISBN 978-80-272-7653-0

Contents

If you wish to escape, if you would go to faraway places, then go to sleep and dream. For sometimes that is the only way....

All along the line of machines, the men's hands and arms worked like the legs of spiders spinning a web. They wound wire and hammered bolts, tied knots and welded pieces of steel and fitted gears. They did not look at each other or sing or whistle or talk or laugh.

And then-he made a mistake.

Instantly he stepped back and a trouble shooter moved into his place. The trouble shooter's hands flew over the controls.

The trouble shooter finished and the workman took his place. His arms moved ceaselessly again.

He was a tall man, slim and wiry, his dress identical to that of the others-grey coveralls that fit like tights.

Suddenly a red light flashed in his eyes and he began to tremble. He took two steps backward. The trouble shooter moved into the empty space.

The man stood for a moment, like a soldier at attention, turned and walked smartly toward the mouth of a corridor.

The silence was like a motion picture with a dead sound track. There was only motion-and him walking down the line of machines where the hands reached out, working, working.

In the corridor now, he looked straight ahead, marching. The walls glowed like water beneath a shallow sea.

He raised his arm, felt the door strike and the heel of his hand; felt it swing open; saw the desk suspended from the ceiling by luminous, silver chains.

A man with a massive, white-maned head and a pink, smiling face rose from behind the desk. His suit was like that of a general.

"Well, Twenty-three." The Superfather stared down at the dossier on his desk. "Two mistakes in three months. Too bad. Just when you were on your way to the head of the machine room."

"I don't know what's the matter with me," said Twenty-three.

"I'm afraid we'll have to drop you back to a less responsible position."

"Of course."

The Superfather looked up quickly. "You accept this? No depression? No threat of suicide?... You *are* in bad shape." He handed a packet of cards to Twenty-three. "Put these in your dream machine tonight. Go to your new job tomorrow."

Twenty-three stood motionless, staring over the other man's shoulder.

The Superfather sat down. "Tell me about the dreams you have when you don't use the machine."

Twenty-three made a quick decision. He couldn't tell him he didn't use the standard dream cards anymore. And he certainly couldn't tell about the *other* dream cards he'd been getting from the little man he'd met on the street. He'd simply answer the factual truth to the question that had been asked.

"Well," he said, as though he were confessing a crime. "I dream I'm walking in the city. It's dark. I feel like I've got to find something. I don't know what. But the feeling's very strong. All of a sudden I notice the city's empty. There're just buildings and streets and a faint glow of light. And it comes to me that everybody's dead and buried. Then I know what I'm looking for. I've got to find something alive or I'll die too. So I start running around, in and out buildings, up and down streets. But there's nothing. I'm breathing so hard I think my heart's going to burst. Finally I fall down. I feel myself beginning to die. I try to get up but I can't! I try to yell! I've got no voice! I'm so afraid, I can't stand it! Then I wake up."

The Superfather frowned. "Incredible. Several other cases like yours have turned up in the last month. We're working on them. But yours is the worst yet. You had such high capabilities. Your tests showed, when you first began to work, ten years ago, that you were capable of going to the head of your production line. But you're not doing it. Also your normal dreams should correspond to the ones on the cards. And they don't....Are you using the standard cards every other night?"

Twenty-three lied. "Yes."

"And the nights you don't use them, you have a dream like the one you just told me."

"That's right."

"Incredible." The Superfather shook his head. "It just doesn't add up. As you know, you get the prescribed dreams every other night and that's supposed to condition your mind to dreaming those same dreams, by itself, on the nights you don't use the machine. The prescribed dreams merely show you the true way of life. And when you're on your own you're supposed to follow that way of life whether you're asleep or awake. That's what the dream machine is for. I'm sure you're aware of all this?"

"Yes," said Twenty-three. "Yes."

"Now we Superfathers *never* have to use the dream machines. We're so filled with the way of life they advocate and it's become such an integral part of us, we simply *are* what our prescribed dreams are. And the more successful a person is in the city, the less he has to use the dream machine. Now you have to use it every other night. That's entirely too much for a man of your potential. You realize this, of course.

"Oh I do," said Twenty-three shaking his head sadly.

"Well now," said the Superfather, "that means something's wrong. *Very* wrong." He rubbed his chin, thinking. "Your prescribed dreams show you working faster and faster on the machines, going on month after month year after year, with one hundred percent accuracy. They show you happy in your work, driven by ambition on up to the end of your capabilities. They show you contented there to the end of your working life." He paused. "And you're *doing* just the opposite ...I suppose your wife is-concerned?"

Twenty-three nodded.

"After all, the marriage center assured her your index was right for her. *Her* sleep cards were coordinated with yours. The normal dreams of both of you, without the machine, should be identical.... Yet you come up with this horror-running through the city, alone, falling, dying."

Twenty-three's mouth twitched.

"Well." The Superfather stood. "If you can't adjust to normal, we'll simply have to send you to the pre-frontal lobotomy men. You wouldn't want that."

"Oh no!"

"Good!" The Superfather held out another packet of cards. "Use these *tomorrow* night. It's a concentration pattern which should be dense enough to make you dream of being, well-perhaps even President, eh?"

"Yes." Twenty-three hesitated.

"Well?" said the Superfather.

"I'd —like to ask a question."

The Superfather nodded.

"What-what use," went on Twenty-three, "is all this-work being put to-that we do-along the machine lines-every day? We don't, seem to really be *making* anything. Just working."

The Superfather's eyes narrowed. "You're kept busy. You get paid. You live. The city is here. That's all. That's enough."

"Yes, sir. Thank you, sir." Twenty-three turned abruptly, marched to the door and stepped into the empty, silent corridor.

Twenty-three looked up at the glowing dome of the city that curved away to the horizon. He wondered if there really was a white ball beyond it sometimes and tiny dots of light, set in blue black. And at other times did a ball of fire flame up there, giving light and heat and life? And if there was this life and light up there, *why* the great dome over the city? *Why* the factories and machine lines replacing it section after section, generation after generation? The slabs that the workers fused together this year and the next and the next, pushing back this life and light and heat. Why not let it pour down into the city and warm all the people? Why not go to the space out there and the depth and freedom? Why this great shell that closed them away? For the sake of the Superfathers maybe? And the Superfathers-plus? For the sake of the ones, like himself maybe who worked and built? For the sake of them, so they wouldn't become dangerous maybe and tear the great wall down and rush out into whatever was beyond? Why else?

But it could be all a farce. They could all be working in the great dome because they didn't know what was beyond. Who could know if they'd never been beyond?

And so they were held under the domes with the buildings and the machines that carried them all around in the city; held with the plumbing and the theatres and all the intricate mechanisms that spoke to them and fed them, that washed them and poured thoughts into their minds, that healed them when they were sick and rested them when they were tired. The same as they were held with the great dome. Held and shackeled with the replacing of parts that didn't need replacing; the making over and over again of the tiny and large pieces of the mechanisms and the taking of the old mechanisms and the melting of them or smashing of them to powder so that this dust or molten metal could be fashioned again and again into the same pieces that they had been for so many thousands of years. All this to keep them busy? All this to keep something outside that was supposed to be destructive because once it had been so five thousand years ago or ten or fifty? All this because that was the way it had been for as long as the hundreds and the thousands of years that history had been recorded?

He walked on through the silence, dimly aware now of the people moving about him, of the automobiles rolling past, as though moved by some invisible force. He passed row upon row of movie theatres that called to him with invisible vibrations. He turned away.

Where was the little man?

He stopped, moving only his eyes. After a moment, he saw the little man step out of a shop-front and stand waiting. Twenty-three, a cigarette in his mouth, walked over and asked for a light. The little man touched a lighter to the cigarette, at the same time dropping a packet of cards into Twenty-three's pocket.

Twenty-three moved on. He felt the pounding of his heart. If only his wife were asleep so he would not have to wait to look at these new cards.

As he walked, his thoughts cried out against the silence. He glanced suspiciously from side to side. If only he could hear the sounds of the city. But except for human voices and music, the city had always been silent. The human voices spoke only words written by the Superfathers, and the music came from records that had been composed by them-all this back when the city had first come into being. Other than these sounds there could be only the quiet all around. No chugging motors or scraping footsteps. No crashing engines in the sky, or pounding of steel on stone. No shrieking of factory whistles or clanging steeple bells or honking automobile horns. None of this to pluck and pound at nerves, to suggest that this place was not the most soothing and gentle of all places to be in. There were no winds to swirl and moan away into the distance. The chirp of birds had long since been stilled, and so had the patter of rain and the crash of thunder. There must not be any of these sounds either to lure the imagination into some distance where danger and excitement might be waiting.

Now he was walking toward the door of his apartment house. It swung open. Thirty seconds later he stopped before another door. It too swung open.

His wife stood in the middle of the room, between two traveling bags. He moved slowly toward her and stopped just out of arm's reach.

"What's this?" He gestured toward the bags. "Where're you going?"

She stared at him for a long moment, her face set. She was of his height and build and wore a suit the same light grey as his. Their hair cuts were identical, their faces sharp featured and pale. They might have been brother and sister-or two brothers, or two sisters.

"I'm going to the marriage center."

"What for?" He had tried to inject surprise into his voice. But the tone was listless.

"The Superfather called about your dream."

Twenty-three turned away, lighted a cigarette. He should beg her to stay, should promise to change. But the silence was in him, like a sickness.

"A terrible thing's happening to you. I don't want any part of it." She picked up the bags. "When you come to your senses, you know where to reach me.... *If* I haven't already made another contract, I *might* come back to you."

She hesitated at the door.

"There's one thing I don't understand. You haven't begged me to stay. You haven't broken down. You haven't threatened suicide." She paused. "It's standard procedure, you know. It might even make me decide to wait awhile."

"I don't want you to stay," he said. He felt a shock of surprise. It was as though a voice had spoken from behind him.

He watched the door shut between them.

Dressed in his pajamas, he stood beside the metal tube, in which for so many years he had slept his regulation sleep and dreamed his regulation dreams. There was something of the finely made casket about this tube-the six foot length and three foot diameter; the lid along its top and the dull shine of the metal and the quiet of it, as though it were asleep and lying in wait for a tired body to bring it awake so that it could put the body to sleep and live in the dreams it would give to the sleeper.

Beside his own tube stood its twin, where his wife had also slept and dreamed through the years.

Leaning slightly forward, he felt the press of metal against his hip bones, felt the tube roll an inch with his weight. He rested one hand on the metal top, felt its warmth and smoothness, was aware of its cleanness, like that of a surgical instrument.

Now he glanced at the glistening black panel that stood two feet high at the tube's head; quickly checked its four illuminated dials and three gleaming arrows and at the same time raised his hand to drop the cards into the softly glowing slot at the panel's top.

Suddenly his hand stopped.

He bent forward.

What was this? A feeling of strangeness. Vague. Like sensing some subtle change in a picture that has hung for twenty years above the fireplace in one's home.

He drew closer, squinting. The dials and meters seemed to be the same as they had yesterday and the day before and the year before.

And yet?

The dials. Larger? By a fraction? And the tiny gleaming arrows of the meters. Barely longer? And the marks on the dials and meters? One extra each, very faintly, like a piece of hair.

He was very still for a long moment. Then he moved around the foot of his own sleeping tube, pushed between the two and stood at the head of the other one.

He checked its dials and meters. They were as they had been for many years. He stepped back to the panel of his own and pressed a button. As the glistening metal top rose, silently, he ran his hand around the yawning interior, felt the downy softness and the body-like warmth. Then his hand touched a pliable metal plate. That should not be there. He stood back, remembering the workmen who had come into the house that morning for the routine checkup of the tubes. His wife had already left for work and he had just stepped through the door when they had met him in the corridor. They had gone on into the rooms and he had sensed vaguely that something was wrong. Then he had put the feeling out of his mind and gone to his work.

Now suddenly, he turned to the illuminated four inch square panel above the door, read April 15, 2563. The workmen had checked a day early. He frowned. Either the Superfather had ordered the machine changed, which was highly improbable, because every object in the city was standardized and any change would upset the established order, or the workmen were tied up with the man who had given him the different dream cards....In any event he had to sleep in the tube that night and he definitely wanted to dream the dreams on the cards he had just gotten from the man on the corner.

He dropped the cards into the slot at the top of the panel, climbed into the tube and pressed a button. The top closed over him, like a hand. He lay still, feeling the warm clasp wash over his body. There was darkness and silence and a cool motion of antiseptic air. He could try the first dream. If it wasn't right, he could shut it off and sleep without dreams.

He pressed another button.

Silence.

The sound of his regular breathing.

Then a sighing came into his mind, and a green haze. The sighing became a soft breeze; the green, tree-covered hills rolling off to the horizon. He relaxed, aware in a fading, sinking part of his consciousness that the machine worked as usual. He would dream and wait and hope....

And so the wind was breathing across the land from off a vast stretch of blue water, which broke along a sandy beach in foamy white breakers. The surf thundered all through his body. The wind brushed against him like a great, purring cat. He looked up at the blue sky and seemed to feel himself rising and sinking, both at the same time, up into its depths. As his sight touched the sun there was an explosion of brightness which blinded him. He turned away then to the rolling green sea of hills, saw the trees bending from the surge of wind and heard the rustling of leaves.

And then a deep voice moved through his mind.

"Outside the city," it said, "all this exists. During the terrible burning of the Earth back in the wars of its antiquity, the city was built as a place of life for those who yet lived. But those people were not aware that the Earth would come alive again and they made the city so that no death could enter it from without and no life could escape from within. And they turned away from the Earth and lived only with the city so that it became their universe-to all but a

15

very few of us. We still held a faint awareness of what the Earth had been-this passed down to us for many generations, in whisperings, by the wise ones of our people, back in the beginning of the city. And in those times, we had been in the city too long, for thousands of years. We knew that there must be freedom beyond the walls, if we could get through. But the walls were thick and high and without a flaw, making a sky over us. We worked for five hundred years on a machine to get us through the wall. Now a few of us have succeeded and more will follow us to the freedom out here in the good land. There is room for everyone here, there are no boundaries and no ceilings and no walls anywhere. And you may join us some time in the near future, if you wish."

Twenty-three sighed in his sleep.

Now a great city faded into his mind. There were long, tree lined streets and buildings, some built in rising spirals, some in spreading squares, others in ovals, domes and curved half circles. The wind wandered among the buildings and the bursts of green. People, dressed in white, flowing robes or black tights, walked the streets. He could hear their footsteps on the stone or grassy walk, could hear the hum of vehicles rolling along the streets or flying through the air. They were long and streamlined or short and round, or they were curved like gondolas or squat like saucers. And they were moving at many speeds. Yet there was order. And the air was sweet and clean. A black line of clouds was rising across the horizon. Soon there would be lightning and thunder and cool rain.

The deep voice touched him again. "This is the city that can be. A city of life, open to the sky and the earth, a city in which people can find and follow their own lives. After the wars, the cities were built to shut out the death of Earth. But the Earth has come to life again. And so can the cities."

The silence came while the picture changed and Twenty-three stirred, waiting.

A figure grew in his mind, wavered, and became a woman. Twenty-three saw the long body and the softness; saw the flowing hair and the smile as she watched him. He saw the gentleness in her face; saw a strength under the softness, like the storm that lies below the charged quiet of a summer evening. Her lips moved.

"Paul. Dream your dreams for *us*." The words seemed to fall on him. He trembled and cried out. And he felt a violent stirring in his body and a breaking away as though he had flung himself through the walls of a tomb.

The picture blew away while the voice continued: "She is a woman, not a woman who half resembles a man." A pause. "When you wish to leave the city, ask for the final card. You are welcome."

There was silence and darkness. Twenty-three stirred. He opened his eyes. The glow from the city outside filtered into the room through the translucent walls. He lay motionless. Paul. He was Paul. Not Twenty-three. A man with a name. Wonder came into him, and a sense of strength, and a willingness to remember without fear.

His mind ran back to the first mistake, almost a year past. He remembered the horror of failure then and the terror at his being subjected to a mistake. He remembered the inference from the Superfather that there might be a bad strain in his blood line. He remembered taking the dream cards that were to have set him straight, that were to have shown him working over the machines with super speed, moving up along the production line to its pinnacle and on up to the position of Superfather and on up to Superfather-plus and on up to the place of Father of The City. But the cards had been sabotaged, so that from them into his mind had come the dreams of the trees and the oceans and the green earth spreading off to the horizon and the expanse of blue sky.

And then the words had directed him to the little man who had given him the cards on the street corner. They had known him, the words had said, through what was called telepathetic screening, for ones suitable to leave the city. He was one of those chosen, because he, like a few others, had been unable to adjust completely to the demands of the city. He was one of those in whom a rebellious nature had been passed down from generation to generation, by attitudes and acts of his ancestors, by a word spoken here and one there, by an intangible reaching out toward the sky and the green growing things and the need to understand who and what he was. But in him now this feeling was weak and close to death and would die in him if it were not brought out into life of the Earth.

Now the memories receded; he lay motionless, listening to his breathing and his heartbeat, feeling his body press against the softness that held him.

Suddenly a shaft of light fell on him through the transparent square. Opening his eyes, he saw his wife's face staring down at him.

She moved her hand. The lid of the tube raised. He lay watching her, feeling naked and, for a moment, helpless.

"I talked for a long while with your Superfather," she said. "I feel better. He told me you'd promised to take the prescribed dreams tonight."

Twenty-three turned his face away from her.

She began to undress.

"I'm going out for a walk." He stepped from the machine.

She watched him dress, her look a mixture of curiosity and fright.

When he left it was as though he were leaving an empty room and she watched him as though he were not quite human.

The glow of the city was all around him as he walked toward the corner where the little man stood. The telepathic advertisers reached out from the places of entertainment, pulling at him. The voices enveloped him for a moment so that he almost turned back to them. But then he saw, in his mind, his arms working over the machines, saw them make a wrong motion that smashed a gear, saw the flashing red light and the heavy, expressionless face of the Superfather. He was aware that his memory would be erased and the skies, and the ocean, and the green hills. His name would be gone. Paul would die. And the city would be his tomb.

Quickly he turned down a side street, saw the small figure leaning against the corner of the building.

Walking rapidly toward him, as though he were being chased, he saw the lean, ruddy face smile and the deep, blue eyes look at him; heard the voice gently say:

"Welcome, Paul."

"The last card," said Twenty-three.

The little man handed it to him, quickly. "Good luck. Turn the dials one extra point on the control panel. Our men have made the machine ready. It's time now."

Twenty-three thrust the card into the inner pocket of his jacket. So that *was* it. They *had* changed the machine.

"One extra point," he repeated, glancing up and down the street.

"And remember," said the little man. "Destroy all the cards you've used before. They were designed particularly for you. If you don't make it across to us, the Superfathers will use the cards against you."

Twenty-three whirled around. The little man had gone. Twenty-three suddenly felt weak. My God! The other cards! Left in the machine! If his wife —!

He stood very still for a long moment, then he ran!

The door to his apartment swung open. The room beyond was empty. A light shown faintly. He stood for a moment, listening. Silence. He stepped to the bedroom. The top of his wife's sleeping tube was closed. He could see her face through the transparent square, could hear her quiet breathing.

In one quick, silent motion, he stepped to the side of his own tube, pulling the last card from his pocket, and dropped it into the glowing slot at the top of the black control panel. Then he turned the dials to the extra point.

Several minutes later he pressed the button at the bottom of the control panel. The top opened. At the same moment, he heard a step behind him. He whirled around. The Superfather stood in the doorway. At his back hovered the dark bulks of two other men. Twenty-three felt his muscles lock. He saw the Superfather's dead smile and then his wife stepping down to the floor and hurrying to the side of the Superfather.

"Those pictures," she said, shuddering. "They were so-strange."

The Superfather held his eyes on Twenty-three but spoke to the woman. "Thank God you were strong. It was commendable of you to call us."

"I don't know what made me look at his dreams," she cried. "Maybe it was when I asked him if he'd taken the prescribed dreams and he didn't answer....Anyway, I tested his machine. It was insane!"

"Dreams made by some twisted mind," the Superfather said. "Remember. They've no real existence. Nothing lives or moves outside the city. There were old myths but they've been dead for countless generations." He paused. "Where *are* the pictures?"

"I burned them."

"Good." He motioned to the men behind him. They came forward and stood on each side of Twenty-three.

"Twenty-three," said the Superfather, "we may have to erase your memories and your present individuality." He cleared his throat. "Our records show that some two thousand people have disappeared in the last five years. Your case has much to do with it....Where'd you get the new cards?"

Twenty-three was silent.

The Superfather pulled out a pack of cards. "Before we leave this room, you'll be a different man. If you tell us," —he waggled the cards in his right hand —"this'll be your new life. You'll have dreams of outdoing every man on the machine lines and fix your body so you'll have the capacity to do it. You *will* do it. You'll become a Superfather. You'll burn to excel them. You'll push on up, become a Superfather-plus. You'll work with ideas, ways of increasing efficiency, pushing the workmen faster and faster. And you'll find ways of conditioning them to meet the greater and greater demands for speed. The city and people'll be at your fingertips. There'll be rooms of marble and gold for you. Soft carpets and buttons to push that'll give you any desire instantly. You'll *have* everything and *be* everything!" He paused and took a deep breath. "All this'll be yours if you'll tell us where you got the cards, without forcing us to probe your mind with the electric-scalpel...."

With an effort, Twenty-three raised his eyes to the Superfather's face.

"And if I don't tell you?"

"Moving a lever back and forth twice a minute hour after hour, year after year. Living in a bare cubicle. No entertainment. No desires." He paused. "And no *memories*."

Twenty-three looked over the Superfather's shoulder. The last card, he thought, is in the machine. Escape from the city. They said that, from outside. I've got to know. No matter what they put in the machine, that card will show first. Even if it's only for ten seconds or thirty or sixty, or however long —I'll know.

"No," he said, "I won't tell you...."

The woman gasped and hid her face. The Superfather, scowling, made a motion.

The two dark men took hold of Twenty-three. They lifted him into the tube.

The Superfather dropped the second pack of cards into the panel and pressed the button. The top closed silently, like a mouth.

Twenty-three's eyes closed; his body waited.

For an instant-blackness, and silence, like a moment after death, or a moment before birth. Then twilight, or dusk, over an ocean. A sky of pale blue. A shine on the gently surging waters. A scent of clean air. Sea spray. The cool sound of wind. Then a man's voice, deep and flowing: "You know that there is no entrance or exit to this city. It is sealed off and will always be so. But the dream machine in which you lie has been changed by our agents inside the city. The last card you dropped into it is different from the others. These changes have been made so your dream will become a reality. Your mind will be transmitted to us here among the hills and under the trees and by the ocean. And a new body, that we have grown, artificially, from all the elements, a body like the one you will leave behind, will be waiting for you. You need not be afraid."

Twenty-three felt himself moving forward. Sight and hearing and sensation, without a body. Time dropping away, like a forgetting of yesterday and tomorrow. There was only this moment. And then he felt the great humming surging power of the machine, like an ocean rushing him toward some unseen shore. He was caught in a gigantic tingling shock wave, and felt like a tremendously outsized torch, lit and flaming, and carried, still burning, in the green tide of sizzling electricity. The machine screamed. The machine chanted. The machine raved. Dimly, he heard his wife cry, and above him felt the Superfather scrabbling at the machine, the guards shouting. The machine shrieked and the great tidal wave of power jolted and flung him, white-hot kindling, through air, through sky, up and down! Down upon a white shore, upon creaming sands, leaving him to quiet, to silence, to a pulling away of the tide....

Now the scent of sea came strong into him. He heard the crash and roar of surf and the rustling of leaves and the sweep of wind. There were bird songs and the cries of animals. He saw the spread of rolling hills, saw a stream searching its way among great rocks and swelling and rolling full into a river and the river flowing and sinking into the sea. He felt the earth upon his feet and the touch of grass. Breezes, heavy with green from the land eddied all around him and filled his body and washed him. He heard his name-saw people coming toward him saying, "Welcome." He felt their arms, embracing him. He saw an open city growing among the hills. Its buildings rolled away with the hills of the Earth and became a part of the Earth. The people took him by the hand and led him toward it speaking to him of no one hurting the other, and no one locked in a cell and all the walls of this world outside, tumbled down....

He was happy and repeated the name they spoke to him.

"Paul."

Back in the city, in the room, the wife cried out.

The Superfather, too, seeing the strange look on the face of the man inside the chrysalis of the dream-maker, quickly touched the button that raised the lid. He bent down and took the wrist of the cold man lying there.

"Dead."

"Are you sure?"

The Superfather bent still further down and listened to the chest, and the wife came close, and they both stood there, half-bent. The mouth of the dead man was open and the Superfather listened for any faint whisper of breath. The wife listened. They both looked at each other for a long time.

Because, from the open mouth of the cold man lying there, faintly, far away, and fading slowly into silence, they heard quiet laughter, and the sound of many birds and voices, and trees rustling in the late afternoon. Then it was gone and no matter how the two people bending there waited and listened, it was like putting their ear to a white stone.

It's not always "The Truth shall set you free!" Sometimes it's "Want of the Truth shall drive you to escape!"
And that can be dangerous!

Mryna Brill intended to ride the god-car above the rain mist. For a long time she had not believed in the taboos or the Earth-god. She no longer believed she lived on Earth. This paradise of green-floored forests and running brooks was something called Rythar.

Six years ago, when Mryna was fourteen, she first discovered the truth. She asked a question and the Earth-god ignored it. A simple question, really: What is above the rain mist? God could have told her. Every day he answered technical questions that were far more difficult. Instead, he repeated the familiar taboo about avoiding the Old Village because of the Sickness.

And consequently Mryna, being female, went to the Old Village. There was nothing really unusual about that. All the kids went through the ruins from time to time. They had worked out a sort of charm that made it all right. They ran past the burned out shells of the old houses and they kept their eyes shaded to ward off the Sickness.

But even at fourteen Mryna had outgrown charms and she didn't believe in the Sickness. She had once asked the Earth-god what sickness meant, and the screen in the answer house had given her a very detailed answer. Mryna knew that none of the hundred girls and thirty boys inhabiting Rythar had ever been sick. That, like the taboo of the Old Village, she considered a childish superstition.

The Old Village wasn't large-three parallel roads, a mile long, lined with the charred ruins of prefabs, which were exactly like the cottages where the kids lived. It was nothing to inspire either fear or legend. The village had burned a long time ago; the grass from the forest had grown a green mantle over the skeletal walls.

For weeks Mryna poked through the ruins before she found anything of significance —a few, scorched pages of a printed pamphlet buried deep in the black earth. The paper excited her tremendously. It was different from the film books photographed in the answer house. She had never touched anything like it; and it seemed wonderful stuff.

She read the pamphlet eagerly. It was part of a promotional advertisement of a world called Rythar, "the jewel of the Sirian Solar System."

The description made it obvious that Rythar was the green paradise where Mryna lived-the place she had been taught to call Earth. And the pamphlet had been addressed to "Earthmen everywhere."

Mryna made her second find when she was fifteen, a textbook in astronomy. For the first time in her life she read about the spinning dust of the universe lying beyond the eternal rain mist that hid her world.

The solid, stable Earth of her childhood was solid and stable no longer, but a sphere turning through a black void. Nor was it properly called Earth, but a planet named Rythar. The adjustment Mryna had to make was shattering; she lost faith in everything she believed.

Yet the clock-work logic of astronomy appealed to her orderly mind. It explained why the rain mist glowed with light during the day and turned dark at night. Mryna had never seen a clear sky. She had no visual data to tie her new concept to.

For six years she kept the secret. She hid the papers and the astronomy text which she found in the Old Village. Later, after the metal men came, she destroyed everything so none of the other women would know the Earth-god was a man.

At first she kept the secret because she was afraid. For some reason the man who played at being god wanted the kids to believe Rythar was Earth, the totality of the universe enveloped in a cloud of mist. She knew that because she once asked god what a planet was. The face on the screen in the answer house became frigid with anger-or was it fear? —and the Earth-god said:

"The word means nothing."

But late that night a very large god-car brought six metal men down through the rain mist. They were huge, jointed things that clanked when they walked. Four of them used weapons to herd the kids together in their small settlement. The two others went to the Old Village and blasted the ruins with high explosives.

Vaguely Mryna remembered that the metal men had been there before, when the kids were still very small. They had built the new settlement and they had brought food. They lived with the children for a long time, she thought-but the memory was hazy.

As the years passed, Mryna's fear retreated and only one thing became important: she knew the Earth-god was a man. On the fertile soil of Rythar there were one hundred women and thirty men. All the boys had taken mates before they reached seventeen. Seventy girls were left unmarried, with no prospect of ever having husbands. A score or more became second wives in polygamous homes, but plural marriage had no appeal for Mryna. She was firmly determined to possess a man of her own. And why shouldn't it be the Earth-god?

As her first step toward escape, Mryna volunteered for duty in the answer house. For as long as she could remember, the answer house had stood on a knoll some distance beyond the new settlement. It was a square, one-room building, housing a speaking box, a glass screen and a console of transmission machinery. Anyone in the settlement could contact god and request information or special equipment.

God went out of his way to deluge them with information. The simplest question produced voluminous data, transmitted over the screen and photographed on reels of film. Someone had to be in the answer house to handle the photography. The work was not hard, but it was monotonous. Most of the kids preferred to farm the fields or dig the sacrificial ore.

A request for equipment was granted just as promptly. Tools, machines, seeds, fertilizers, packaged buildings, games, clothing-everything came in a god-car. It was a large cylinder which hissed down from the rain mist on a pillar of fire. The landing site was a flat, charred field near the answer house. Unless the equipment was unusually heavy, the attendant stationed in the house was expected to unload the god-car and pile aboard the sacrifice ores mined on Rythar.

God asked two things from the settlement: the pieces of unusually heavy metal which they dug from the hills, and tiny vials of soil. In an hour's time they could mine enough ore to fill the compartment of a god-car, and god never complained if they sometimes sent the cylinder back empty. But he fussed mightily over the small vials of Earth. He gave very explicit directions as to where they were to take the samples, and the place was never the same. Sometimes they had to travel miles from the settlement to satisfy that inexplicable whim.

For two weeks Mryna patiently ran off the endless films of new books and unloaded the god-car when it came. She examined the interior of the cylinder carefully and she weighed every possible risk. The compartment was very small, but she concluded that she would be safe.

And so she made her decision. Tense and tight-lipped Mryna Brill slipped aboard the god-car. She sealed the lock door, which automatically fired the launching tubes. After that there was no turning back.

The dark compartment shook in a thunder of sound. The weight of the escape speed tore at her body, pulling her tight against the confining walls. She lost consciousness until the pressure lessened.

The metal walls became hot but the space was too confining for her to avoid contact entirely. Four narrow light tubes came on, with a dull, red glow, and suddenly a gelatinous liquid emptied out of ceiling vents. The fluid sprayed every exposed surface in the cubicle, draining through the shipment of sacrifice ores at Mryna's feet. It had a choking, antiseptic odor; it stung Mryna's face and inflamed her eyes.

Worse still, as the liquid soaked into her clothing, it disintegrated the fiber, tearing away the cloth in long strips which slowly dissolved in the liquid on the floor. Before the antiseptic spray ceased, Mryna was helplessly naked. Even her black boots had not survived.

The red lights went out and Mryna was imprisoned again in the crushing darkness. A terror of the taboos she had defied swept her mind. She began to scream, but the sound was lost in the roar of the motors.

Suddenly it was over. The god-car lurched into something hard. Mryna was thrown against the ceiling-and she hung there, weightless. The pieces of sacrifice ore were floating in the darkness just as she was. The motors cut out and the lock door swung open.

Mryna saw a circular room, brightly lighted with a glaring, blue light. The nature of her fear changed. This was the house of the Earth-god, but she could not let him find her naked.

She tried to run into the circular room. She found that the slightest exertion of her muscles sent her spinning through the air. She could not get her feet on the floor. There was no down and no up in that room. She collided painfully with the metal wall and she snatched at a light bracket to keep herself from bouncing free in the empty air again.

The god-car had landed against what was either the ceiling or the floor of the circular room. Mryna had no way of making a differentiation. Eight brightly lighted corridors opened into the side walls. Mryna heard footsteps moving toward her down one of the corridors; she pulled herself blindly into another. As she went farther from the circular room, a vague sense of gravity returned. At the end of the corridor she was able to stand on her feet again, although she still had to walk very carefully. Any sudden movement sent her soaring in a graceful leap that banged her head against the ceiling.

Cautiously she opened a thick, metal door into another hall-and she stood transfixed, looking through a mica wall at the emptiness of space pinpointed with its billions of stars. This was the reality of the charts she had seen in the astronomy text: that knowledge alone saved her sanity. She had believed it when the proof lay hidden above the rain mist; she must believe it now.

From where she stood, she was able to see the place where the god-car had brought her-like a vast cartwheel spinning in the void. The god-car was clamped against the hub, from which eight corridors radiated outward like wheel spokes toward the rim. Far below the gigantic wheel Mryna saw the sphere of Rythar, invisible behind its shroud of glowing mist.

She moved along the rim corridor, past the mica wall, until she came to a door that stood open. The room beyond was a sleeping compartment and it was empty. She searched it for clothing, and found nothing. She went through four more dormitory rooms before she came upon anything she could use-brief shorts, clearly made for a man, and a loose, white tunic. It wasn't suitable; it wasn't the way she wanted to be dressed when she faced him. But it had to do.

Mryna was pawing through a footlocker looking for boots when she heard a hesitant step behind her. She whirled and saw a small, stooped, white-haired man, naked except for trunks like the ones she was wearing. The wrinkled skin on his wasted chest was burned brown by the hot glare of the sun. Thick-lensed glasses hung from a chain around his neck.

"My dear young lady," he said in a tired voice, "this is a men's ward!"

"I'm sorry. I didn't know—"

"You must be a new patient." He fumbled for his glasses. Instinctively she knew she shouldn't let him see her clearly enough to identify her as a stranger. She shoved past him, knocking the glasses from his hand.

"I'd better find my own-ward." Mryna didn't know the word, but she supposed it meant some sort of sleeping chamber.

The old man said chattily, "I hadn't heard they were bringing in any new patients today."

She was in the corridor by that time. He reached for her hand. "I'll see you in the sunroom?" It was a timid, hopeful question. "And you'll tell me all the news-everything they're doing back on Earth. I haven't been home for almost a year."

She fled down the hall. When she heard voices ahead of her, she pulled back a door and slid into another room —a storeroom piled with cases of medicines. Behind the cartons she thought she would be safe.

This wasn't what she had expected. Mryna thought there might be one man living in a kind of prefab somehow suspended above the rain mist. But there were obviously others up here; she didn't know how many. And the old man frightened her-more than the dazzling sight of the heavens visible through the mica wall. Mryna had never seen physical age before. No one on Rythar was older than she was herself—a sturdy, healthy, lusty twenty. The old man's infirmity disgusted her; for the first time in her life she was conscious of the slow decay of death.

The door of the supply room slid open. Mryna crouched low behind the cartons, but she was able to see the man and the woman who had entered the room. A woman-here? Mryna hadn't considered that possibility. Perhaps the Earth-god already had a mate.

The newcomers were dressed in crisp, white uniforms; the woman wore a starched, white hat. They carried a tray of small, glass cylinders from which metal needles projected. While the woman held the tray, the man drove the needles through the caps of small bottles and filled the cylinders with a bright-colored liquid.

"When are you leaving, Dick?" the woman asked.

"In about forty minutes. They're sending an auto-pickup."

"Oh, no!"

"Now don't start worrying. They have got the bugs out of it by this time. The auto-pickups are entirely trustworthy."

"Sure, that's what the army says."

"In theory they should be even more reliable than —"

"I wish you'd wait for the hospital shuttle."

"And miss the chance to address Congress this year? We've worked too long for this; I don't want to muff it now. We've all the statistical proof we need, even to convince those pinchpenny halfwits. During the past eight years we've handled more than a thousand cases up here. On Earth they were pronounced incurable; we've sent better than eighty per cent back in good health after an average stay of fourteen months."

"No medical man has ever questioned the efficiency of cosmic radiation and a reduced atmospheric gravity, Dick."

"It's just our so-called statesmen, always yapping about the budget. But this time we have the cost problem licked, too. For a year and a half the ore they send up from Rythar has paid for our entire operation."

"I didn't know that."

"We've kept it under wraps, so the politicians wouldn't cut our appropriations."

Their glass tubes were full, and they turned toward the door. "It isn't right," the woman persisted, "for them not to send a piloted shuttle after you, Dick. It isn't dignified. You're our assistant medical director and —"

Her words were cut off as the door slid shut behind them. Mryna tried to fit this new information into what she already knew-or thought she knew-about the Earth-god. It didn't add up to a pretty picture. She had once asked for a definition of illness, and it was apparent to her that this place which they called the Guardian Wheel was an expensive hospital for Earthmen. It was paid for by the sacrificial ores mined on Rythar. In a sense, Rythar was being enslaved and exploited by Earth. True, it was not difficult to dig out the ore, but Mryna resented the fact that the kids on Rythar had not been told the truth. She had long ago lost her awe of the man called god; now she lost her respect as well.

Mryna was glad she had not seen him, glad no one knew she was aboard the Guardian Wheel. She would return to Rythar. After she told the others what she knew, Rythar would send up no more sacrifice ores. Let the Earthmen come down and mine it for themselves!

Very cautiously she pulled the door open. The rim corridor was empty. She moved toward one of the intersecting corridors. When she heard footsteps, she hid in another dormitory room.

This was different from the others. It showed more evidence of permanent occupation. She guessed it was a dormitory for the people who took care of the sick. Pictures were fastened to the curved, metal walls. Personal articles cluttered the shelves hung beside the bunks. On a writing desk she saw a number of typed reports. Five freshly laundered uniforms, identical to the one she had lost in the antiseptic wash, hung on a rack behind the door. Mryna stripped off the makeshift she was wearing and put on one of the uniforms; she found boots under the desk. When she was dressed, she stood admiring herself in the polished surface of the metal door.

She was a handsome woman, and she was very conscious of that. Her face was tanned by the mist-filtered sunlight of Rythar; her lips were red and sensuous; her long, platinum-colored hair fell to her shoulders. She compared herself to the small, hard-faced female she had seen in the supply room. Was that a typical Earthwoman? Mryna's lips curled in a scornful smile. Let the gods come down to Rythar, then, and discover what a real female was like in the lush, green, Rytharian paradise.

Mryna went to the desk and glanced at the typed reports. They had been written by a man who signed himself "Commander in Charge, Guardian Wheel," and they were addressed to the Congress of the world government. One typed document was a supply inventory; a second, still unfinished, was a budget report. (*You won't show a profit next time*, Mryna thought vindictively, *when we stop sending you the sacrifice ore.*) Another report dealt with Rythar, and Mryna read it with more interest.

One paragraph caught her attention,

"We have asked for soil samples to be taken from an area covering ten thousand square miles. Our chemical analysis has been thorough, and we find nothing that could be remotely harmful to human life. Atmospheric samples produce the same negative results. On the other hand, we have direct evidence that no animal life has ever evolved on Rythar; the life cycle is exclusively botanical."

The soil samples, Mryna realized, would be the vials of Earth which the Earth-god had requested so often. Were the Earthmen planning to move their hospital down to Rythar? That idea disturbed her. Mryna did not want her garden world cluttered up with a lot of sick, old men discarded by Earth.

She turned to the second page of the report. "The original colony survived for a year. The Sickness in the Old Village developed only after the first harvest of Rytharian-grown food. It is more and more evident that the botanical cycle of Rythar must be examined before we find the answer. To do that adequately, we shall have to send survey teams to the surface; that requires much larger appropriations for research than we have had in the past. The metal immunization suits, which must, of course, be destroyed after each expedition —"

"And what, may I ask, is the meaning of this?"

Mryna dropped the report and swung toward the door. She saw a woman standing there-another hard-faced Earthwoman, with a starched, white cap perched on her graying hair.

"I must have come to the wrong room," Mryna said in a small voice.

"Indeed! Everyone knows this is command headquarters. Who are you?" The woman put her hand on Mryna's arm, and the fingers bit through the uniform into Mryna's flesh.

Mryna pulled away, drawing her shoulders back proudly. Why should she feel afraid? She stood a head taller than this dried up stranger; she knew the Earthwoman's strength would be no match for hers.

"My name is Mryna Brill," she said quietly. "I came up in a god-car from Rythar."

"Rythar?" The woman's mouth fell open. She whispered the word as if it were profanity. Suddenly she turned and ran down the rim corridor, screaming in terror.

She's afraid of me! Mryna thought. And that made no sense at all.

Mryna knew she had to get back to the god-car quickly. Since the Earthmen had built up the taboos in order to get their sacrifice ores from Rythar, they would do everything they could to prevent her return. She ran toward an intersecting spoke corridor. An alarm bell began to clang, and the sound vibrated against the metal walls. An armed man sprang from a side room and fired his weapon at Mryna. The discharge burned a deep groove in the wall.

So they would even kill her-these men who pretended to be gods!

Before the man could fire again, Mryna swung down a side corridor, and at once the sensation of weightlessness overtook her. She could not move quickly. She saw the armed man at the mouth of the corridor. Frantically she pushed open the door of a room, which was crowded with consoles of transmission machines. Three men were seated in front of the speakers. They jumped and came toward her, clumsily fighting the weightlessness.

Mryna caught at the door jamb and swung herself toward the ceiling. At the same time the armed man fired. The discharge missed her and washed against the transmission machinery. Blue fire exploded from the room. The three men screamed in agony. Concussion threw Mryna helplessly toward the rim again.

And the Guardian Wheel was plunged into darkness. Mryna's head swam; her shoulder seethed with pain where she had banged into the wall. She tried to creep toward the circular room, but she had lost her sense of direction and she found herself back on the rim.

The clanging bell had stopped when the lights went out, but Mryna heard the panic of frightened voices. Far away someone was screaming. Running feet clattered toward her. Mryna flattened herself against the outer wall. An indistinct body of men shot past her.

"From Rythar," one of them was saying. "A woman from Rythar!"

"And we've blasted the communication center. We've no way of sending the warning back to Earth —"

They were gone.

Mryna moved back into the spoke corridor. She felt her way silently toward the circular hub room and the god-car. Suddenly very close she heard voices which she recognized-the man and the woman who had been talking in the supply room.

"You're still all right, Dick," the woman said. "She hasn't been here long enough to —"

"We don't know that. We don't know how it spreads or how quickly. We can't take the chance."

"Then...then we've no choice?" Her voice was a small whisper, choked with terror.

"None. These have been standing emergency orders for twenty years. We always faced the possibility that one of them would escape. If we'd been allowed to use a different policy of education-but the politicians wouldn't permit that. The Wheel has to be destroyed, and we must die with it."

"Couldn't we wait and make sure?"

"It works too fast. None of us would be able to do the job-afterward."

The voices moved away. Mryna floated toward the hub room. She found the air lock and pulled herself into the god-car. The metal lock hissed closed and light came on. Then she knew she had made a mistake. This ship was not the one she had used when she came up from Rythar. The tiny cabin was fitted with a sleeping lounge, a food cabinet and a file of reading films. Above the lounge a mica viewplate gave her a broad view of the sky.

Mryna remembered that the man in the supply room had said he was waiting for an auto-pickup; he was on his way back to Earth. Mryna had taken his ship instead of her own. In panic she tried to open the door again, but she found no way to do it. Machinery beneath her feet began to hum. She felt a slight lurch as the pickup left the hub of the Guardian Wheel.

It swung in a wide arc. Through the viewplate she saw the enormous Wheel growing small behind her, silhouetted against the mist of Rythar. Suddenly the wheel glowed red with a soundless explosion. Its flaming fragments died in the void.

Mryna dropped weakly on the lounge. Nausea spun through her mind. The man had said they would destroy themselves. Because Mryna had come aboard? But why were they afraid of her? What possible harm could she do them? Mryna had left Rythar to discover the truth, and the truth was insanity. Was truth always like this —a bitter disillusionment, an empty horror?

She had something else to say to the people of Rythar now: not that the gods were men, but that men were mad. Believe in the taboos; send up the sacrificial ores. It was a small price to pay to keep that madness away from Rythar.

And Mryna knew she could not go back. With the Wheel gone, she could never return to Rythar; the auto-pickup was carrying her inexorably toward Earth. The scream of the machinery slowly turned shrill, hammering against her eardrums. The stars visible in the viewplate blurred and winked out. Mryna felt a twist of vertigo as the shuttle shifted from conventional speed into a time warp. And then the sound was gone. The ship was floating in an impenetrable blackness.

Mryna had no idea how much time passed subjectively. When she became hungry, she took food from the cabinet. She slept when she was tired. To pass the time, she turned the reading films through the projector.

Most of the film stored in the shuttle covered material Mryna already knew. The Earthmen, clearly, had not denied any information to Rythar. Only one thing had been restricted-astronomy. And that would have made no difference, if Mryna had not found the text in the ruins of the Old Village. The people on Rythar never saw the stars; they had no way of knowing-or caring-what lay above the rain mist.

Mryna was more interested in the history of Earth, which she had never known before. She studied the pictures of the great industrial centers and the crowded countryside. She was awed by the mobs in the city streets and the towering buildings. Yet she liked her own world more-the forests and the clear-running brooks; the vast, uncrowded, open spaces.

It puzzled her that the people of Earth would give the Rytharian paradise to a handful of children, when their own world was so overcrowded. Was this another form of the madness that had driven the people in the Wheel to destroy themselves? That made a convenient explanation, yet Mryna's mind was too logical to accept it.

One film referred to the founding of the original colony on Rythar, a planet in the Sirian System which had been named for its discoverer. Rythar, according to the film, was one of a score of colonies established by Earth. It was unbelievably rich in deposits of uranium.

That, Mryna surmised, was the name of the sacrificial ore they sent up in the god-cars.

The atmosphere and gravity of Rythar duplicated that of Earth; Rythar should have become the largest colony in the system. The government of Earth had originally planned a migration of ten million persons.

"But after twelve months the survey colony was destroyed by an infection," Mryna read on the projection screen, "which has never been identified. It is called simply the Sickness. The origin of this plague is unknown. No adult in the survey colony survived; children born on Rythar are themselves immune, but are carriers of the Sickness. The first rescue team sent to save them died within eight hours. No human being, aside from these native-born children, has ever survived the Sickness."

Now Mryna had the whole truth. She knew the motivation for their madness of self-destruction. It was not insanity, but the sublime courage of a few human beings sacrificing themselves to save the rest of their civilization. They smashed the Guardian Wheel to keep the Sickness there. And Mryna had already escaped before that happened! She was being hurled through space toward Earth and she would destroy that, too.

If she killed herself, that would in no way alter the situation. The ship would still move in its appointed course. Her body would be aboard; perhaps the very furnishings in the cabin were now infected with the germ of the Sickness. When the ship touched Earth, the fatal poison would escape.

Dully Mryna turned up another frame on the film, and she read what the Earthmen had done to help Rythar. They built the Guardian Wheel to isolate the Sickness. Sealed in metal immunization suits, volunteers had descended to the plague world and reared the surviving children of the colonists until they were old enough to look out for themselves. The answer house had been set up as an instructional device.

"As nearly as possible, the scientists in charge attempted to create a normal social situation for the plague carriers. They could never be allowed to leave Rythar, but when they matured enough to know the truth, Rythar could be integrated into the colonial system. Rytharian uranium is already a significant trade factor in the colonial market. An incidental by-product of the Guardian Wheel is the hospital facility, where advanced cases of certain cancers and lung diseases have been cured in a reduced gravity or by exposure to cosmic radiation."

Mryna shut off the projection. The words made sense, but the results did not. And she knew precisely why Earth had failed. When they matured-in those three words she had her answer.

And now it didn't matter. There was nothing she could do. Her ship was a poisoned arrow aimed directly at the heart of man's civilization.

Mryna had slept twice when the auto-pickup lurched out of the time drive and she was able to see the stars again. Directly ahead of her she saw an emerald planet, bright in the sun. And she knew instinctively that it was Earth.

A speaker under the viewport throbbed with the sound of a human voice.

"Auto-shuttle SC 539, attention. You are assigned landing slot seven-three-one, Port Chicago. I repeat, seven-three-one. Dial that destination. Do you read me?"

Three times the message was repeated before Mryna concluded that it was meant for her. She found three small knobs close to the speaker and a plastic toggle labeled "voice reply." She snapped it shut and found that she could speak to the Chicago spaceport.

Her problem was easily solved, then. She could say she came from Rythar. Without hesitation, Earth ships would be sent to blast her ship out of the sky before she would be able to land. But she knew she had to accomplish more than that; the same mistake must not be repeated again.

"How much time do I have?" she asked.

"Thirty-four minutes."

"Can you keep this shuttle up here any longer than that?"

"Lady, the auto-pickups are on tape-pilot. Come hell or high water, they land exactly on schedule."

"What happens if I don't dial the slot destination?"

"We bring you in on emergency-and you fork over a thousand buck fine."

Mryna asked to be allowed to speak to someone in authority in the government. The Chicago port manager told her the request was absurd. For nine minutes Mryna argued, with a mounting sense of urgency, before he gave his grudging consent. Her trouble was that she had to skate close to the truth without admitting it directly. She could not-except as a last resort-let them kill her until they knew why the isolation of Rythar had failed.

It was thirteen minutes before landing when Mryna finally heard an older, more dignified voice on the speaker. By then the green globe of Earth filled the sky; Mryna could make out the shapes of the continents turning below her. The older man identified himself as a senator elected to the planetary Congress. She didn't know how much authority he represented, but she couldn't afford to wait any longer.

She told him frankly who she was. She knew she was pronouncing her own death sentence, yet she spoke quietly. She must show the same courage that the Earthmen had when they sacrificed themselves in the Guardian Wheel.

"Listen to me for two minutes more before you blast my ship," she asked. "I rode the god-car up from Rythar—I am coming now to spread the Sickness on Earth-because I wanted to know the truth about something that puzzled me. I had to know what was above the rain mist. In the answer house you would not tell us that. Now I understand why. We were children. You were waiting for us to mature. And that is the mistake you made; that blindness nearly destroyed your civilization.

"You will have to build another Guardian Wheel. This time don't hide anything from us because we're children. The truth makes us mature, not illusions or taboos. Never forget that. It is easier to face a fact than to have to give up a dream we've been taught to believe. Tell your children the truth when they ask for it. Tell us, please. We can adjust to it. We're just as human as you are."

Mryna drew a long breath. Her lips were trembling. Did this man understand what she had tried to say? She would never know. If she failed, Earth-in spite of its generosity and its courage-would one day be destroyed by children bred on too many delusions. "I'm ready," Mryna said steadily. "Send up your warships and destroy me."

She waited. Less than ten minutes were left. Her shuttle began to move more slowly. She was no more than a mile above Earth. She saw the soaring cities and the white highways twisting through green fields.

Seven minutes left. Where were the warships? She looked anxiously through the viewport and the sky was empty.

Desperately she closed the voice toggle again. "Send them quickly!" she cried. "You must not let me land!"

No reply came from the speaker. Her auto-shuttle began to circle a large city which lay at the southern tip of an inland lake. Three minutes more. The ship nosed toward the spaceport.

"Why don't you do something?" Mryna screamed. "What are you waiting for?"

The shuttle settled into a metal rack. The lock hissed open. Mryna shrank back against the wall, looking out at what she would destroy-what she had already destroyed. A dignified, portly man came panting up the ramp toward her.

"No!" she whispered. "Don't come in here."

"I am Senator Brieson," he said shortly. "For ten years Dr. Jameson has been telling us from the Guardian Wheel that we should adopt a different educational policy toward Rythar. Your scare broadcast was clever, but we're used to Jameson's tricks. He'll be removed from office for this, and if I have anything to say about it —"

"You didn't believe me?" Mryna gasped.

"Of course not. If a plague carrier escaped from Rythar, we would have heard about it long before this. The trouble with you scientists is you don't grant the rest of us any common sense. And Jameson's the worst of the lot. He's always contended that the sociologists should determine our Rytharian policy, not the elected representatives of the people."

Mryna broke down and began to cry hysterically. The senator put his hand under her arm-none too gently. "Let's have no more dramatics, please. You don't know how fortunate you are, young lady. If the politicians were as addle-witted as you scientists claim we are, we might have believed that nonsense and blasted your ship out of the sky. You scientists have to give up the notion that you're our guardians; we're quite able to look out for ourselves."

www.ingramcontent.com/pod-product-compliance
Lightning Source LLC
Chambersburg PA
CBHW071231130626
46555CB00004B/1935